WANTED
in connection with
possible Rhyme Criming.

Jon Burgerman

Jon is an award-winning artist who has created murals, sculptures, toys, apparel, and now picture books, all with his trademark playful, bright aesthetic. His art is collected worldwide by several institutions including the Victoria and Albert Museum in London. Born in the UK, Jon currently lives in Brooklyn with his wife and fellow artist, You Byun.

Visit Jon at jonburgerman.com and @jonburgerman.

Dedicated to my parents

Needed: large snake
...ogs

OXFORD
UNIVERSITY PRESS

Great Clarendon Street, Oxford OX2 6DP

Oxford University Press is a department of the University of Oxford. It furthers the University's objective of excellence in research, scholarship, and education by publishing worldwide. Oxford is a registered trade mark of Oxford University Press in the UK and in certain other countries

Text and Illustrations © Jon Burgerman 2017

The moral rights of the author and illustrator have been asserted
Database right Oxford University Press (maker)

First published 2017

British Library Cataloguing in Publication Data

Data available

ISBN: 978-0-19-274950-5
ISBN: 978-0-19-274951-2 (eBook)

1 3 5 7 9 10 8 6 4 2

Main text set in Burgerman 1.7 with the permission of the author

Printed in China

Paper used in the production of this book is a natural, recyclable product made from wood grown in sustainable forests. The manufacturing process conforms to the environmental regulations of the country of origin.

Missing
Monty the Mouse

Likes
cheese
nibbles

Reward contemplated

Will t...
clogs.

me asap!

 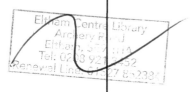
Rhyme Crime

Jon Burgerman

Once upon a time,

a thief
committed a crime.

Everything he stole
was replaced with
a **rhyme.**

Hammy's brand new hat
was swapped for a...

Gumpop's lovely head
became a slice of ...

bread.

Oh, crumbs!

Arney's comfy chair
was switched for a...

bear.

Tootle's loyal dog
was taken for a...

Moomoo's fancy clogs
were swapped for some...

Gertie's pretty house
was now a giant...

Marlow's happy smile
became a...

crocodile.

Dingle's mighty sneeze

was swapped for stinky...

Blue's yummy cake
was taken for a...

snake.

Sleepy Boomer's brain
was switched for a ...

train.

The thief took Tumble's orange,
and swapped it with a...

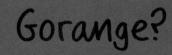

jail.

What terrible luck.

I'm truly stuck!

But by the very next day

the thief had run....